To Penelope,
my original cupcake princess
—P.C.

To my mother,
who always kept the cookie jar full of tasty homemade treats
—M.H.

Published in the United States by Random House Children's Books, a division of Random House, Inc., New York.

Random House and the colophon are registered trademarks of Random House, Inc.

Visit us on the Web! www.randomhouse.com/kids

Educators and librarians, for a variety of teaching tools, visit us at www.randomhouse.com/teachers

Library of Congress Cataloging-in-Publication Data
Cartaya, Pablo.
Tina Cocolina: queen of the cupcakes / by Pablo Cartaya and Martin Howard ; illustrated by Kirsten Richards. — 1st ed.
p. cm.
Summary: Tina Cocolina is a cupcake searching for her perfect topping so that she can compete in the annual Cream of the Top Cupcake contest.
Includes recipes for cupcakes and toppings from award-winning pastry chef Martin Howard.
ISBN 978-0-375-85891-8 (trade) — ISBN 978-0-375-95891-5 (lib. bdg.)
[1. Cup cakes—Fiction. 2. Icings, Cake—Fiction. 3. Individuality—Fiction. 4. Contests—Fiction.] I. Howard, Martin. II. Richards, Kirsten, ill. III. Title.
PZ7.C24253Tin 2010 [E]—dc22 2008034175

MANUFACTURED IN CHINA
10 9 8 7 6 5 4 3 2 1
First Edition

Tina Cocolina
Queen of the Cupcakes

by Pablo Cartaya and Martin Howard
illustrated by Kirsten Richards

RANDOM HOUSE NEW YORK

At the Gingersnap Academy for Rising Cupcakes in southern Charleston, most of the cupcakes had found their toppings.

Tina Cocolina had not. What was worse, the Cream of the Top Cupcake contest was tonight, and everyone knew that cupcakes without toppings could not compete!

Tina's classmate Candyce Cremiere, last year's Cream of the Top Cupcake Queen, found her spicy buttercream topping while scratching out a recipe during snack time!

Billy Barry Blue, a red velvet cupcake from Marietta, found his frosting while rolling in a patch of ripe berries on a dare!

Even Carmella du Chocolat, a French exchange cake who was a whole year younger, found her triple berry fudge swirl while playing the viola in music class one day.

But poor Tina Cocolina had not the slightest idea what to wear as her topping. She searched everywhere.

She wandered through the peanut butter brownie patch. But peanut butter just wasn't *her.*

She trotted to the chocolate fudge sauce stream and dipped her head in, hoping the fudge would stick.

Sticky as it was, it didn't stick to her!

Then Tina went to the weeping caramel tree and looked up into its branches, glistening with delicious, gooey sauce. What an *excellent* topping it would make!

But the branches stuck to her head and she couldn't get down! She had to kick and swing herself every which way to pull herself free.

It was only two hours until the contest, and still Tina Cocolina had not found her topping. Sadly, she dragged herself home.

She went into the kitchen and flung her pastry bag onto the counter. Mamma Cocolina was busy making supper.

Mamma Cocolina was a beautiful cupcake. When she was a girl, she had won the Cream of the Top Cupcake contest three times! She had found her favorite topping—raspberry buttercream with toasted almonds—while cheering for the school team, the Mixed Fruit Tarts.

"What's the matter, sweetie?" Mamma asked.

"Mamma, why haven't I found my topping yet?" Tina asked.

"Don't worry. Every cupcake finds a topping when the time is right. I'm sure you will find yours. Why don't you get washed up for supper? Papa will be home soon."

Tina went upstairs, still worried.
She washed her hands and brushed the loose crumbs from her face.
There was barely a speck of topping on her head.

Tina went into her room and spotted a bright pink berry balloon in the corner.

She had an idea!

Tina grabbed the balloon and painted it with dark chocolate swirls. She tied it on her head with a licorice shoestring.

Then she ran into Mamma and Papa's bathroom and dipped it in the melted white chocolate they kept in their silver washbasin.

She had found her topping!

She ran downstairs.

Papa was very surprised. “Sweetie, is that a new school project you’re wearing?”

“No,” Tina said, twirling. “I have found my topping!”

Mamma and Papa looked at each other and smiled. “That’s wonderful,” Papa said. “I’m very glad you did. It’s quite a topping.”

Tina smiled proudly and took her seat at the table. Her topping dangled above her head.

Suddenly, she heard a buzzing sound.

A sugar fly had flown in!

Warily, Tina watched it as it flew around and around the table and landed right on her topping!

The sugar fly chomped down on the pink berry balloon and . . .

POP!

"I'll never win now," Tina said tearfully as Mamma and Papa wiped the chocolate from her face.

"Why don't you clean yourself up and we'll take you to the contest," Mamma said.

"Don't worry. There's always next year," said Papa.

But Tina didn't want to wait until next year.

At the competition, most of the other cupcakes were getting ready backstage. Cupcakes without toppings had to be helpers. Tina didn't want to be a helper. She wanted to be Queen.

Candyce said, "Tina, since you don't have a topping yet, why don't you be my helper?"

"No, thank you, Candyce. I'm going to find my topping—you'll see!"

"Why don't you just give up, Tina!" Candyce said.

But Tina wasn't giving up.

"Maybe you can use this for inspiration." Candyce laughed.

Tina looked at Candyce's leftover snack, some wilted strawberry leaves and a shriveled old banana skin, and stormed off.

She was just about to fling them into the trash when she got an idea. A brilliant idea. A wonderful, delicious idea.

She ran outside into the strawberry fields. There she picked three perfect ruby-colored strawberries as they glistened in the moonlight.

Next she went to the banana tree. The nice, ripe bananas were too high for her to reach! She grabbed a chocolate rock and flung it into the biggest, ripest bunch.

The bananas fell right into Tina's arms. She quickly peeled the bananas, mixed them with the fresh, glowing strawberries, and formed a shiny, creamy wave on top of her head.

Tina zoomed back into school just as Mr. Taffee was saying, "And the winner of this year's Cream of the Top Cupcake Crown is . . ."

"Wait!" Tina yelled as she strode down the aisle with her strawberry banana cream swirl glowing on her head.

A hush fell over the auditorium.

Then suddenly, the room erupted into thunderous applause.

Mr. Taffee ripped the envelope in half and declared, “Miss Tina Cocolina is the winner of this year’s Cream of the Top Cupcake contest!”

Mr. Taffee placed the silver-sprinkle crown on Tina’s head, careful not to muss her perfect wave.

All the other cupcakes cheered.

Tina Cocolina was the Queen!

Cream of the Top Cupcakes and Crowns!

Tina Cocolina's Winning Recipes

An adult's help in the kitchen is heartily recommended.

Tina Cocolina
A Sweet, Plain Vanilla Cupcake

Makes 18–20 medium cupcakes or 36–40 mini

1/2 c. butter
1-1/4 c. sugar
3 eggs
1-1/2 tsp. vanilla extract
1 tsp. salt
2 c. flour
1 tbsp. baking powder
1 c. milk

In a bowl with an electric mixer, cream together butter, sugar, eggs, vanilla, and salt until light and fluffy. Sift together flour and baking powder, then add alternately with milk. Blend together until smooth. Scoop into lined cupcake pans filled 2/3 full. Bake at 350 degrees for 20 minutes or until springy to the touch.

Carmella du Chocolat
A Devil's Food Cupcake

Makes 24 medium cupcakes or 48 mini

3/4 c. water
3/4 c. cocoa powder
3/4 c. butter
2 c. sugar
1 tsp. salt
1 tsp. vanilla extract
3 eggs
2-1/2 c. cake flour
1 tsp. baking powder
1 tsp. baking soda
1 c. buttermilk

In a small pot, bring water to a boil. Remove from heat and whisk in cocoa powder. Cover and set aside.

In a bowl with an electric mixer, cream together butter, sugar, salt, and vanilla. Add eggs and continue creaming until light and fluffy.

Sift together cake flour, baking powder, and baking soda. Add alternately with buttermilk. Add cocoa-and-water mixture and mix. Scrape bowl well with rubber spatula and continue mixing until thoroughly combined. Scoop into lined cupcake pans filled 2/3 full. Bake at 350 degrees for 20 minutes or until springy to the touch.

Billy Barry Blue
A Southern Red Velvet Cupcake

Makes 24 medium cupcakes or 48 mini

1/2 c. butter
1-1/3 c. sugar
2 eggs
1 tsp. salt
1 tsp. vanilla extract
2-1/2 c. flour
2 tbsp. cocoa powder
1 c. buttermilk
3 tbsp. red food coloring
1 tsp. baking soda
1 tbsp. vinegar

In a bowl with an electric mixer, cream together butter, sugar, eggs, salt, and vanilla until fluffy.

Sift together flour and cocoa, then add alternately with buttermilk.

Add red food coloring. Put baking soda on top of batter, pour vinegar over it, and mix until combined and smooth.

Scoop into lined cupcake pans filled 2/3 full. Bake at 350 degrees for 20 minutes or until springy to the touch.

Candyce Cremiere
A Rich Sour Cream Vanilla Pound-Cake Cupcake

Makes 18–20 medium cupcakes or 36–40 mini

- 1 c. butter
- 1 c. sugar
- 1/2 tsp. salt
- 1 tsp. vanilla extract
- 4 eggs
- 1-3/4 c. cake flour
- 1 tsp. baking powder
- 1/2 c. sour cream

In a bowl with an electric mixer, cream together butter, sugar, salt, and vanilla. Add eggs one at a time, beating well after each.

Sift together cake flour and baking powder. Add slowly, and mix in sour cream last.

Scrape bowl well with a rubber spatula and mix until smooth. Scoop into lined cupcake pans filled 2/3 full. Bake at 325 degrees for 20–25 minutes or until a toothpick comes out clean when stuck in a cupcake.

Creamy Chocolate Topping

Enough for 24 medium cupcakes

8 oz. chocolate chips
2 tbsp. butter
3/4 c. heavy cream
2 tbsp. sugar

Place chocolate chips and butter in a bowl.

In a pot, bring cream and sugar to a boil and pour over chocolate chips and butter. Stir until smooth.

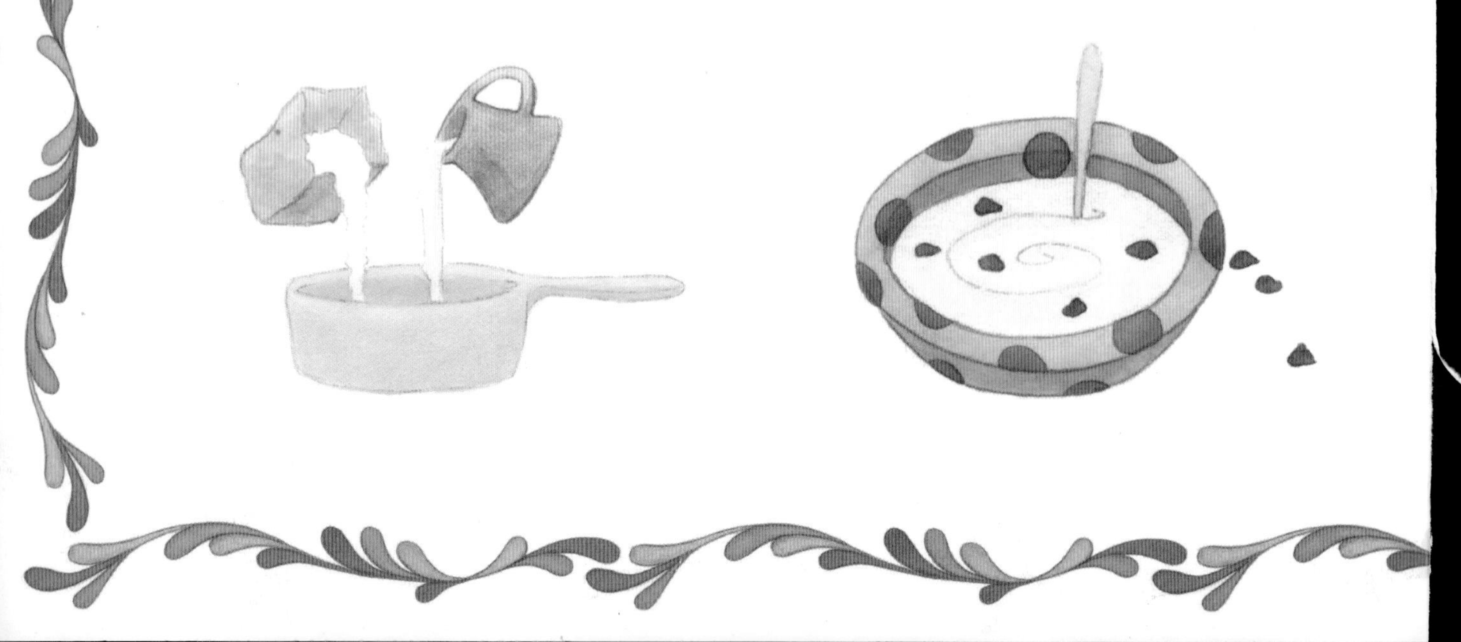

Buttercream

Enough for 24 medium cupcakes

4 egg whites
2/3 c. sugar
1 c. butter, room temperature
1 tsp. vanilla extract

Whisk together egg whites and sugar in a bowl.

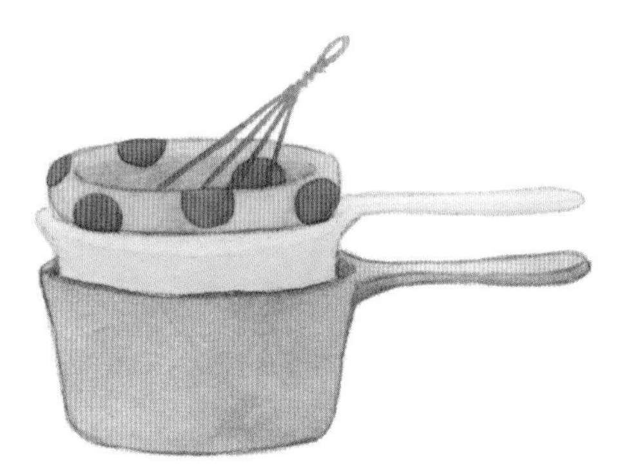

Place bowl in a double boiler on low heat. Whisk occasionally until sugar is dissolved and mixture is very warm, about 150 degrees.

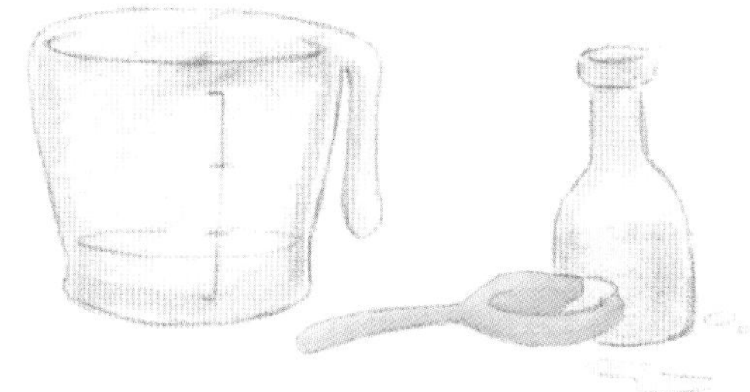

Remove from double boiler and whip with mixer on high speed until stiff peaks form. Put mixer on a lower speed and add butter in small pieces. Add vanilla and mix until smooth. For banana buttercream, add 1/2 tsp. banana extract and a few drops of yellow food coloring.